COWBOY
With a Camera

Erwin E. Smith, Cowboy Photographer
Story by Don Worcester

This publication is made possible by a grant from the Erwin E. Smith Foundation.

All photographs in this book are in the Amon Carter Museum in either the Mary Alice Pettis Collection or the Erwin E. Smith Collection of the Library of Congress on deposit, unless otherwise noted.

First Edition

ISBN 0-88360-091-9
Library of Congress Catalog Card Number: 98-85992

Worcester, Don
Cowboy with a Camera, Erwin E. Smith: Cowboy Photographer

Summary: A historical account of cowboy life on the open range as told through the photographs of Erwin E. Smith (1886-1947) and story by Don Worcester (b. 1915).

Front cover: *Boys of the LS Ranch in Texas, lingering at the chuck wagon, listening to the range boss tell stories, 1908.*
Front flap: *Photographer Erwin E. Smith, rearing his horse, 1910.*
Back cover: *A young wrangler on the Three Block Ranch, New Mexico, 1908.*

The Amon Carter Museum was established through the generosity of Amon G. Carter, Sr. (1879-1955) to house his collection of paintings and sculpture by Frederic Remington and Charles M. Russell; to collect, preserve, and exhibit the finest examples of American art; and to serve an educational role through exhibitions, publications, and programs devoted to the study of American art.

TABLE OF CONTENTS

Erwin E. Smith and his mount overlooking the Palo Duro Canyon in Texas.

◇

My name is Erwin E. Smith. The E stands for Evans, in case you were wondering. When I was growing up in North Texas in the early 1900s, I always knew I wanted to be a cowboy. On my summer vacations, I visited my uncle's ranch in Foard County on the Red River. The day of trail herds to Kansas had ended in the 1880s, but I remember seeing the herds on their way to Texas markets, and to me those cowboys on their horses seemed bigger than the Texas sky. I read about cowboys in adventure stories all the time, and I couldn't wait until I could actually ride with them.

Well, that day did come around. And when it did, I helped the cowboys **round up** stray cattle, and they taught me how to ride and rope with the best of them. I even had my own brand, the Bar Diamond Bar, which is at the top of this page. All in all, I guess you could say I had my wish come true.

Erwin E. Smith at age 21, 1907.

Photographer Erwin E. Smith eating a mid-morning snack of canned tomatoes, JA Ranch, Texas.

When I was a teenager, my mother gave me my first camera and I started taking pictures. My camera was a lot bigger and heavier than the cameras of today. It used **glass plates** instead of rolls of film, and this made it even heavier! I usually had to put it on a **tripod** to keep it steady while I took pictures.

The photos I took helped me remember all the details of the **cowpunchers'** clothing and gear. When I went away to art school in 1905, I learned how to paint and sculpt the scenes in my photographs. I continued my cowboy work during the summers and took lots more pictures. I soon realized that this wild way of life was changing as the range was fenced, and I didn't want it to be forgotten. So I decided to work as fast as I could to take more pictures of the old ways before they were gone forever. I took photographs on lots of the biggest ranches in North and West Texas, where there were still miles of **open range** and they worked cattle the old way. I even went over into New Mexico and Arizona for more. I wanted to show the real cowboy, the one who wasn't at all like the ones in **dime novels.**

These photographs I took show the way we did things back around 1910. Each picture tells a story, and I'm glad I had the chance to take them when I did. Through photographs and stories we can see the old-time cowboy as he really was – a working man on horseback.

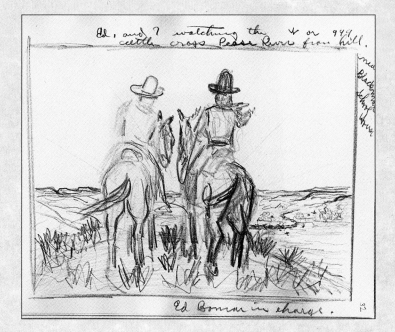

Ed Bomar in charge. Graphite sketch, Nita Stewart Haley Memorial Library.

Cowboys

First, let me tell you a little about how the cowboys came to be. The cowboy was the product of the open range and the **trail drive**, before the day of barbed-wire fences. In Texas, long before my time, cattle roamed freely most of the year and became as wild as deer. The men who rounded up these cattle and drove them to market came to be called cowboys, and they had to do a lot of hard riding. They learned to rope from the Mexican *vaqueros*, the Mexican cowboys who were the first cowboys in Texas. From the 1860s to the 1880s, millions of Texas cattle were driven north to the railroads in Kansas, and the Texas cowboys who drove them there became well known and admired.

Most of the cowboys I knew were Anglo-Americans who might well have come to Texas from any state in the Union. Men from Europe and the British Isles were also drawn to the cattle ranges, among them lots

Cowboys around the wagon, Spur Ranch, Texas.

of Scottish and Irish immigrants. Most cowboys were young men, although there were always some boys and a few old-timers among them. And in my day, there were hardly any cowgirls at all.

African-American cowboys getting ready for rodeo in Bonham, Texas.

Because Texas was once part of Mexico, many early cowboys were Hispanic Texans, or *Tejanos*. Numerous others were African-American, both former slaves and descendants of slaves. At one time there were at least four thousand black cowboys in Texas, and I'm sure there were. Some of them acquired cattle of their own and became ranchers. At **roundup** time, these black cowboys would gather all their **beeves** into a herd, then drive it up the trail to market. Because of their great skill in handling horses and cattle, some *Tejano* and black cowboys became well known and highly respected.

One of the best-known black cowboys was Bill Pickett, the son of former slaves. He was credited with inventing steer wrestling, or **bulldogging,** which would go on to become a featured rodeo event.

Of course, cowboys were expected to be able to do most jobs that involved handling cattle and horses. Like anything you set out to do, though, these skills were developed over time, and each cowboy wound up doing what he was best at doing. Less experienced cowboys looked after the horses or rode behind the herd. Those cowboys with the most experience and wisdom became either the **trail bosses** or **roundup bosses.** I admired them for the way they looked over the whole operation. Old cowboys who could no longer work the cattle but still loved life on the open range often became cooks.

Monclavio Lucero,
Mexican bronc buster,
"working one out"
in the LS Ranch corral,
Texas.

And then there were the **bronc busters.** Bronc busting was a special job on most ranches. It took a unique kind of cowboy to break the half-wild horses off the range, for some were real hard buckers.

Monclavio Lucero being thrown by a bronc, LS Ranch, Texas.

Ranchers left their young horses on the range until they were four years old and mature enough to work cattle. Then they hired professional bronc busters, many of them *Tejanos* or Mexicans, to ride each one several times until it quit bucking. The busters did not spend any time "gentling" the animals; they made sure everything was tied tightly, and climbed on! The horses usually went wild when first saddled. As these photographs show, bronc busters on the LS Ranch were in for hard riding. Even after the animals were turned over to cowboys, some of them were still difficult to ride and handle. It was up to the cowboys to train them.

Square Knot

The cook was the first to rise each morning, long before dawn, to prepare breakfast. We usually groaned when we heard him rattling pots in the dark, knowing we'd soon have to **turn out.** On the trail, he prepared a breakfast of delicious **sourdough biscuits**, beef or bacon, and a big pot of coffee.

JA Ranch cook inspecting his stew, Texas.

Often there was a wind blowing while the cook was preparing a meal. Anyone foolish enough to ride up to the **chuck wagon** on the windward side would raise a cloud of dust. The cook would cuss him out in strong and colorful language. Because they had to rise so early, cooks were usually cranky, or pretended to be. But we didn't mind. As hungry as we always were from hard work and long days, we were grateful to the cook for the job he did – cranky or not!

oys who wanted to be cowboys, but who were too young to handle cattle, were often hired as horse **wranglers.** Early in the morning, the cook would rouse the wrangler, who rubbed his eyes and yawned as he sleepily rode out to drive in the *remuda,* Spanish for "relay of saddle horses." These **saddle horses,** or **cowponies** as they were often called, were the cowboys' work horses. They were allowed to graze at night, and the wrangler had to have the *remuda* back at camp before the cowboys finished breakfast and were ready to go to work.

A young wrangler on the Three Block Ranch, New Mexico.

There's a popular song still sung today, "Little Joe the Wrangler," about a lad who tried to help stop a stampede at night during a storm. He was killed when his running horse fell into a ravine.

Cattle

Every cowboy's life revolved around cattle – "cows" they called them. At first, Texas ranchers raised mainly Texas **Longhorns,** which were slow to grow. The steers had to be left on the range until they were four years old before they were sold to market. Otherwise, they were too small and wouldn't bring much money.

A Longhorn steer, the "symbol of Texas," about to be released after being doctored, OR Ranch, Arizona.

In the days of open range and free grass, letting them feed longer didn't matter much. But when ranges were fenced and grass was limited, ranchers began raising other, faster-developing breeds they could sell in two years. By the time I became a cowboy, most of the big ranches had upgraded their cattle by crossing them with white-faced **Herefords** or other breeds. I still saw a few Longhorns, but they were a disappearing breed. Like most of the old-timers, I hated to see them go. It was in the trail-driving days that they became the very symbol of Texas.

Zack Burkett and Ysabel Gurule of the LS Ranch in Texas, coming to the rescue of a cow wedged under an overhanging rock on a dangerous trail.

I soon learned that cows could get into all kinds of trouble, and that it was up to us to save them. In this photograph on the LS Ranch in Texas, the **range boss** and a Mexican cowboy are rescuing a cow. She had gotten herself trapped under an overhanging ledge and couldn't get to her feet. If left there, she would have died. You can see that the well-trained cowpony is keeping the **lariat** tight while the men struggle with the cow. Like all cowponies, it had been taught to stand still when its rider dropped the reins, and it knew to keep the rope tight. Cooperation between cowboys and their mounts was vital for successful work.

Lariat

15

The name for unbranded cattle came from Texan Samuel Maverick, who received a herd in payment of a debt. The calves had not been branded for several years. When Maverick sold the herd, the new owner had them and all the unbranded animals found over a wide area rounded up. He claimed they were *all* his because they had been "Maverick's," and the name came to mean any unbranded cattle.

Each ranch had its own **brand,** and I got to know many of them. A brand on a cow told you whose animal it was, and it discouraged theft. They were necessary, too, because unbranded cattle

Placing the LS brand on a white calf, LS Ranch, Texas.

a year or older were considered **mavericks,** which meant they had no owner. Any rancher could brand and claim them. Some men in the early days got their start in the ranching business by branding mavericks.

Most of the year the cattle roamed freely on the range, so they were never what I would call tame. Every spring, they were all rounded up so the new calves could be branded while they were still small and easy to bulldog and hold down.

W restling calves down was some of the hottest, dirtiest work I ever saw, and it kept up one after the other until all were marked. It was important not to miss any of the new calves, for next year they were larger, stronger, and much more difficult to handle.

Cowboys worked in teams during branding time. A few of the best ropers **lassoed** the calves and pulled them to the fire. There, two **flankers** caught each calf, threw it to the ground, and held it. Then another cowboy took the hot iron and marked the calf's hide with the rancher's brand. Where several herds were mixed together, the cowboys gave each calf the same brand as its mother.

Working a herd, three ropers keep a set of branders and flankers busy with the hot iron, Spur Ranch, Texas.

Although cowboys and horses worked together at branding time, the calves rarely cooperated. Sometimes their mommas interfered. Cowboys on cowponies and men on the ground had to be alert for kicking calves and their mothers' horns. Cows recognized their calves by their scent, and so it was important that they stayed close together at branding time. Cowboys sometimes had to lead lost calves back to their mothers, like this cowboy is doing.

A young calf following a horse, looking for its mother, Shoe Bar Ranch, Texas.

Jimmy Cain, waiting with a lariat while another cowpuncher ropes a longhorn "outlaw" steer to doctor him, OR Ranch, Arizona.

Sometimes, steers managed to hide from roundup crews for years, and they became known as **outlaws.** They were older, larger, and stronger than others, and they were determined to remain free. They were difficult and dangerous to approach or handle, impossible for a single cowboy to round up. In the case of this huge outlaw steer on the OR Ranch in Arizona, it was necessary for two cowboys to rope him. They brought a small herd of tame cattle and released him into it, then drove them to a pen. His outlaw days were over. Some of these outlaws took a bunch of us to run down and rope.

Horses

The cowboy had no better partner or closer friend on the open range than his cowpony. The first Texas cowponies were **mustangs,** wild descendants of the horses the Spaniards brought to the Southwest. There weren't many pure mustangs left when I rode the

A bad sign, Matador Ranch, Texas. When a cowpony was found without its rider, cowboys knew there had been trouble and would begin searching for the lost rider. The loose lariat suggests a roping accident.

range. Like the Longhorns, they had been crossed with larger breeds. Except for their small size, mustangs made ideal cowponies: smart, strong, and able to run hard for a long time. The half-mustang cowponies that I rode still had these qualities. To produce larger cowponies than the pure mustangs, ranchers crossed mustang mares with stallions of other breeds. These were usually Quarter Horses, Thoroughbreds, or Morgans. Some were also bred to heavy draft horses, such as Percherons, which originated in France.

On roundups and trail drives each cowboy had a **string,** or group of six or more cowponies in the *remuda* for his exclusive use. Some of them were often only half-broken, and cowboys didn't make pets of them. Each cowboy usually had a favorite, though, and these cowponies were often pampered. But pampered or not, handling half-wild cattle required cowponies as well as riders that knew what to do around cattle. It's a fact that the cowboy and the cowpony had to make a very good team. Many a cowboy owed his life to his cowpony's ability to sense danger when racing after stampeding cattle in the dark. And of course, a cowpony needed to be cared for, just like anything else.

Jake Rains gives his pet horse "Comanche" a sourdough biscuit, Spur Ranch, Texas.

Boot and Spur

Emory Sager roping mounts from the *remuda* in a rope corral, Shoe Bar Ranch, Texas.

There were few pens on the range or trail, so *remuda* horses were taught to respect a rope corral. A rope corral could be set up by cowboys simply holding lariats tied together in a circle. We used it a lot on roundups, and it really worked. Cowponies were not trained to let a man walk up to them on the range. That would make them easy to steal. So every time one of us wanted to use a horse from our string in the *remuda*, we had to lasso it in the rope corral.

Not all cowboys were expert ropers, though. So to save time, the boss would sometimes ask a cowboy to name the mount he wanted, and then rope it for him. Like I said, the trail and roundup bosses were men of greater experience and wisdom than most cowboys. "Widow Maker" was a favorite name for troublesome cowponies. Even after they'd been roped, lots of times just getting in the saddle was a chore!

The "usual morning fight." Edwin Sanders (Erwin Smith's cousin) saddling up "Puddin' Foot," a Percheron cross on a Spanish mare, ED Ranch, Texas.

On his Apache campaigns in Arizona, General George Crook perfected the use of pack-mule trains for cavalry troops. No matter how rough the country, the nimble pack mules, carrying 250-pound packs, could go anywhere the cavalry went. They could also keep up with the cavalry day after day. No matter how hard the pursuit, the troopers always had food and ammunition close at hand. An Apache actually said one time that they were always "very discouraged" when they saw a pack train coming.

Tightening the saddle on a pack horse, Three Circle Ranch, Texas.

On parts of some ranges, especially in Arizona and New Mexico, the land was too rough for the chuck wagon to accompany the roundup crews. At such times it was necessary to use pack horses. So cowboys used the Mexican *aparejo,* or packsaddle, and tied the pack on with the famous "diamond hitch." I must admit I never learned how to tie one.

A Matador Ranch "stray man" taking the *remuda* and a pack horse up a rough trail to the Spur range to claim any mavericks belonging to the Matador outfit, Texas.

WORK ON THE RANGE

Roundup

In the spring and fall, neighboring ranchers sent their crews, chuck wagons, and *remudas* to work together on the roundup – and that was always a heap of cowboys and a lot of work. They had to **comb** an enormous area, one part at a time. Each morning, these cowboys mounted horses that could run for a long time. These were their "long" horses, tough animals that were often hard to manage and couldn't be used for other work. Most long horses were hard buckers, so every morning during roundup time was like a rodeo, and you can bet we all wanted to watch that for sure! Long horses could easily run thirty miles or more as the riders drove all of the cattle to a central holding ground. I found these roundups exciting and worked on as many as I possibly could.

"Pink" Murray, roundup boss of the OR outfit, "telling off" his men for the day's work, OR Ranch, Arizona.

Mat Walker, roundup boss for the Matador Ranch, on "Doodlebug," picking out his Matador brand at the roundup, Texas.

On the **spring roundup** each rancher's crew, along with representatives from more distant ranches, searched all the herds for cattle bearing their brands. They would separate out the new calves and brand them before they got too large. After this, some men drove their herds back to the home ranges. The next day, the process was repeated. This continued for several months until the whole, vast range had been worked. Some ranges were thousands of acres big, and it seemed like we'd never get to the end of them.

Mat Walker and his horse "Doodlebug," cutting out a fat cow from the rest of the herd, Matador Ranch, Texas.

On the **fall roundup,** the cowboys gathered all of the cattle at various holding grounds on the vast range. The purpose was to separate the beeves from the herd. These were the full-grown cattle ready to be trailed to market. Because they had been rounded up only a few times, they ran at the sight of a man on horseback. Each day it required hard riding by cowboys on tough horses to round up a herd for cutting.

While cowboys held the herd together, the cutting-horse riders went to work. **Cutting horses** were the elite of the cowponies, and cutting-horse men were the most skillful of the cowboys. Cutting horses had to be intelligent, extremely agile, and well-trained. To us cowboys, nothing was smarter than a cutting horse. A sheepdog was second, and a college graduate third.

A real cutting horse turning on a dime, "Doodlebug" and Mat Walker "cutting one out," Matador Ranch, Texas.

The cutting-horse rider rode slowly among the cattle so as not to startle them. Then he indicated the animal he wanted removed from the herd. The cowpony did the rest, gradually pushing the cow or steer to the edge of the herd. The most difficult part was forcing the animal away from the others. Dodging and turning, it tried hard to get around the horse and rider. But the quick cowpony could always push the animal far enough away so that the other cowboys could drive it off to the market herd.

The Trail to Market

Starting a trail herd north near the southern Arizona border.

In the old days, Texas cattle were sold by class. The same price was paid for all acceptable **yearlings,** all two-year-olds, and so forth. At the **railheads** in Kansas, however, beeves were sold by the pound. The heavier the beef, the more profit to the owner. For this reason, trail cattle were allowed to graze for several hours each morning to put on weight. The rule was never to let them take a step in any direction but north.

A trail herd headed for shipment from Lubbock, Texas.

When the cattle finished grazing each morning, we trailed them to the place the trail boss had selected for the noon break. The chuck wagon and *remuda* were already there, and half of the riders ate hastily while the others held the herd. Then they caught fresh horses and returned to the herd so the other cowboys could eat. Seeing your relief coming at a lope was always a welcome sight. In the afternoon, we trailed the cattle to the place the boss had selected for camp. We usually traveled about twelve miles each day.

The Chisholm Trail, which many herds followed from South Texas to central Kansas in the trailing days, was named for Indian trader Jesse Chisholm. The first herds to central Kansas followed his wagon tracks through Indian Territory, which today is Oklahoma.

Dust of the drags.

Trail herds always raised a long cloud of dust. The **drag riders,** those who brought up the rear, were always coated with thick dust. Since no cowboy wanted to eat dust every day, the drag riders were usually young boys who wanted to become cowboys. Luckily for me, I never had to ride drag.

On the way north to Kansas, the trail crossed a number of rivers, any one of which might be flooded. It was at such times that good lead steers were most valuable, for when they plunged into the river, the other cattle readily followed them.

Some lead steers, like Charles Goodnight's "Old Blue," were never sold. They made many trips up the trail and back. When the herd reached the bed ground each night, Old Blue went to the chuck wagon where the cook gave him sourdough biscuits. When Goodnight stopped trailing cattle, he gratefully retired Old Blue on his ranch in Palo Duro Canyon.

Putting a herd of cattle across the Canadian River in Texas.

DANGERS OF THE SEASONS

A lonely fence rider combing the range during a bitterly cold "blue norther," ED Ranch, Texas.

In the era of the open range, before the invention of barbed wire in the mid-1870s, cattle could easily stray. Much of the time **line riders,** who lived in dugouts on the boundaries of a ranch, kept the cattle from straying. After the range was fenced in, **fence riders** would ride the long rows of barbed wire, looking for breaks that needed mending. But when **blue northers** struck in winter, there was little any cowboy could do in the bitter cold. Being a line or fence rider in winter was not a job that I was eager to try. The heavy snow and sleet could kill any man or animal that was unable to reach shelter. Since I rarely visited any ranch during the winter, I never had to ride through a norther, but I heard plenty of stories about them. They were bad news. At such times, the cattle drifted miserably before the storm. Looking for grass, they had to keep wandering or starve.

On the West Texas plains, where powerful gales and blue northers made life miserable and hazardous in the winter, **dugouts** such as this one on the huge Matador Ranch were typical. They enabled cowboys to survive the frigid winters. Most dugouts were built into a hillside, almost like a cave. Like this one, they were at least partially shielded from the cold by earthen walls on three sides.

Hanging on the crude wall of this Matador dugout are a wolf skin and elks horns. A horseshoe is nailed over the door for good luck. Beside the door is a water bucket and basin, and above these hangs a much-used towel. Alongside the cabin is a water barrel. In the foreground are saddles, blankets, and a lariat.

Hunting season at hand, Matador Ranch dugout, Texas.

35

A windmill on the Two Buckle Ranch, Texas.

Dave Carter, Spur Ranch cowpuncher, on "Butterbean," watching the herd come down to water, Spur Ranch, Texas. The dark bandanna about his throat is for protection from the sun and wind.

N o matter how tall or nutritious the grass, where there was no surface water there was no hope of raising cattle and horses. Because large areas of the West Texas plains had no rivers, creeks, springs, lakes, or ponds, they were difficult even to cross on horseback. I read about early exploring parties, military and civilian, that suffered and even died from thirst. The Comanches and Kiowas, who had crossed these plains on their way to raid in Mexico, learned over the years every place where water was to be found. Eventually, ranchers, cowboys, and exploring parties obtained the same priceless information.

W indmills changed all of this, I'm glad to say, and so the waterless areas were made habitable for humans and animals. A well, a windmill, and a **stock tank** made it possible for cattle to graze over a large area within daily walking distance of water. In areas where there were rivers, creeks, or lakes, water became a problem only in times of severe droughts. When we moved cattle from one part of the range to another

in hot weather, we cowboys drove them to water wherever it was found along the way. We'd water our cowponies and, using the curved brims of our hats, scoop up water for ourselves – even if it was warm or muddy.

Tom King, Matador Ranch cowboy, drinking from the brim of his hat at a spring in Dutchman Pasture, Matador Ranch, Texas.

DAILY LIFE

Sam Whittaker, wagon cook for the LS Ranch, making breakfast in early dawn, Texas.

A t mealtimes on the trail, cowboys were always hungry. They had to be fed all they could eat three times a day, no matter what the weather was doing. For rainy days, when dry wood for a fire wasn't to be found, the cook kept a supply in a **tarp** slung under the wagon. After dark each night, the cook or wrangler pointed the wagon tongue in the direction of the North Star. Before he rode ahead in the morning, the trail boss glanced at the wagon tongue. It was his compass.

Cowpunchers around the fire, eating barbecued ribs, SMS Ranch, Texas.

Making ready for the day's drive, Three Block Ranch, New Mexico.

Mornings, it was the duty of each cowboy to roll up his blankets in his tarp and tie the roll securely. Then he placed it alongside the chuck wagon, or the **hoodlum wagon** if the outfit had one. If someone failed to place his roll by the wagon, the cook drove off and left it. That night the cowboy had to ride back ten or twelve miles to recover it. He was unlikely to make that mistake a second time. Luckily for me, I was warned in time.

Bedroll

The trail bosses eventually added a **night herder** to the crew to keep the *remuda* from scattering while the other cowboys slept. The night herder often drove the hoodlum wagon on the trail during the day, so he had to catch a little shut-eye at every opportunity. Poor guys – most of the time they looked to me like they were in a daze.

Boy wrangler for the Shoe Bar Ranch in Texas brings in a load of wood. Since no cowboy walked when he could ride, the wrangler looped his lariat around dead branches and dragged them to the chuck wagon.

If the night herder did his job, then the wrangler didn't have to hunt for the grazing cowponies in the morning. This saved some time, but the wrangler's job was still a tough one. Once the cowboys had caught their mounts, the wrangler became the cook's helper. He dried dishes and stowed them in a drawer at the back of the chuck wagon. Then he helped pack Dutch ovens and other camp gear. And when they all stopped at noon or to set up camp for the night, it was the wrangler who gathered wood for the cook's fire.

After the day's work was done, cowboys repaired their gear, wove **cinches**, or read, as these Arizona cowboys are doing on roundup. Cowhands would gather books, when they could, and literally read the pages off of them. Some cowboys used the opportunity to catch a few winks, which was hard to do when the weather was bad. When it rained steadily for days and the ground was covered with water, three exhausted cowboys would lie down in a triangle with their heads resting on each other's ankles.

On the trail, most wounds, injuries, or illnesses pretty much had to cure themselves, with the help of a few simple remedies the cook or the boss had. If injuries kept a cowboy from riding his cowpony, he rode on the wagon until he could be taken to the nearest town.

Odd jobs in camp: Joe Gleen, stray man for the Sulphur Cattle Company, Gleeson, Arizona, and D.W. McFarland, stray man for the Wagon Rod outfit, making a cinch. Under the wagon reading is J.W. Haverty of Fort Huachuca.

Once in a while, when we camped near a good stream, we took a quick dip and scrubbed a bit, then washed our pants and shirts. If there were no tree limbs handy, we laid them on the grass to dry. Most of us had a spare shirt, pants, and underwear. But even so, our clothes got really dirty. At the end of three months on the trail or on roundup, the first thing most cowboys did was buy a new outfit. I didn't take any photos of cowboys going to the bathroom, but I can tell you that wasn't a formal occasion. Much of the time there wasn't a tree in sight, but we never worried about that when nature called.

The JA wagon boss taking a shave. There was rarely enough time for shaving in the morning. The herd started moving off the bed ground at dawn, so cowboys had time only for a hasty breakfast.

ecause their life was one of work and long
hours, cowboys were always eager for
entertainment. They would ride all day to attend a
dance in some schoolhouse. They as willingly
danced till daybreak. When there were no dances
to attend, they staged their own. Booted cowboys
took turns playing the parts of ladies.

Boys of the LS Ranch in Texas, lingering at the chuck wagon, listening to the
range boss tell stories.

omeone usually got out a guitar or fiddle
and played while the rest of us sang or did
shag dances. Usually there was a good
storyteller around, and he would keep us
entertained for hours. He always had an
appreciative audience, and although I found
some of the stories a bit hard to swallow,
I never got tired of listening.

Dancing, unhampered by the lack of women.

Cowboys always enjoyed playing card games such as "seven-up." And if someone owned a pair of dice, they might spread a saddle blanket on the ground for shooting craps.

Cowboys also enjoyed playing jokes or tricks on one another, and they played plenty on me. I found some of their humor a bit rough. But I learned to take the good-natured pranks without losing my temper. I laughed with the rest of them and started figuring on how to get even.

Cards and Dice

Charley Thompson and Ed Bomar playing a game of seven-up, Turkey Track Ranch, Texas.

Four cowpunchers shooting craps on a saddle blanket in roundup camp.

W hen several outfits were together on a roundup, we always had some friendly competition, too. We'd see who the best bulldoggers and ropers were, and each crew usually had a few horses that hardly anyone could ride. Cowboys from each ranch liked to pit their best bronc riders against a rival outfit's worst buckers. I have to admit, I wasn't much for fooling with the bad ones.

Monclavio Lucero, Mexican bronc buster of the LS outfit in Texas, bulldogs a steer.

Texas Rodeo, bronc riding.

A few of the old ways I recorded in my photographs can still be seen today in modern rodeos. Among them are roping contests, bronc riding, and cutting horse events. Others that are more a part of cowboy fun than work are trick roping and bull riding. And there are many cowboys and cowgirls who are skillful in one or more of these events.

Whether they're men or women, cowboys are still with us, that's for sure, but they're a different breed from the ones I got to ride with. I hope my pictures will help you remember and admire them. And I tell you what. If you're ever lucky enough to be sitting on a horse someday, looking out over a wide stretch of open land, and your mind wanders back to dreaming of the old days, remember me, would you? Erwin E. Smith – the cowboy with a camera.

Erwin E. Smith, rearing his horse – and he's not holding onto the saddle horn.

GLOSSARY

Aparejo (op-uh-ray-ho): A saddle of Mexican origin designed for use with pack animals.

Beeves: Full-grown steers ready for market. The heavier the beef, the greater the price paid to the rancher.

Blue norther: A bitterly cold winter storm that sweeps down suddenly from the arctic, bringing ice and dangerously cold winds.

Brand: In the days of the open range, each ranch had its own marking that identified the cattle it owned. This mark was applied to a calf's hide with a hot iron. Branding cattle discouraged theft.

Bronc buster: A cowboy who breaks wild horses to the saddle.

Bulldogging: The process of wrestling a steer to the ground from horseback while both are running full speed.

Chuck wagon: A wagon that carried the food as well as the bedrolls and water barrel. Extra firewood was kept in a tarp underneath the wagon, in case of rain.

Cinch: A strap of woven cotton or horsehair that holds the saddle on the horse's back. A typical stock saddle has a forward cinch and a flank cinch.

Comb: To search a large area in a systematic way.

Cowpony: A strong and agile saddle horse trained for herding cattle.

Cowpuncher: Another word for cowboy. Like "cowpoke," it came from the practice of punching or poking cattle to keep them moving along.

Cutting horse: A saddle horse trained to "cut out" individual animals from a herd.

Dime novel: A paperback novel, cheap and easy to carry. The dime novels that cowboys read were usually about a western theme.

Drag rider: A cowboy who rode behind the herd on the trail drive. Usually a young boy who wanted to be a cowboy, the drag rider made sure no cows fell behind and were lost. It was a very dirty job.

Dugout: Residence of line riders who were stationed on the southern edge of the range to keep cattle from drifting south. Most had earthen walls on at least three sides, and some were dug into a hillside like a cave. This protection provided shelter from the extreme weather on the high plains.

Fence rider: A cowboy who rode along the barbed-wire fence lines, looking for holes to mend.

Flanker: At branding time, two flankers would grab a roped calf, throw it to the ground, and hold it for branding.

Glass plates: This is what an image was captured on with cameras in Erwin Smith's time. In his camera, they were 5 x 7 inches in size.

Hereford: Hardy, red-coated English beef cattle with white faces and markings. Herefords grow faster and larger than Longhorns, making them ready for market sooner and, because they're heavier, making them worth more.

Hoodlum wagon: An additional wagon taken on a trail drive or roundup to carry items the chuck wagon had no room to carry. This allowed the cook to carry more food on the chuck wagon. The hoodlum wagon was usually the mark of a well-to-do outfit or ranch.

Lariat: A long, light rope with a noose to catch livestock or tether grazing animals.

Lasso: To capture with a lariat.

Line rider: These were cowboys who lived on the range in dugouts, closer to the cattle, with the goal of keeping them from straying. In winter months, out-of-work cowboys could "ride the line" from camp to camp, never being refused a meal or shelter.

Longhorn: Cattle with long horns that originated in Spain. The Longhorn is the symbol of Texas.

Maverick: An unbranded range animal over a year old, apparently unowned.

Mustang: A small and hardy horse of the western plains directly descended from horses brought to America by the Spaniards.

Night herder: Each cowboy was required to watch the herd for two to four hours during the night. Night herding required a mount that was sure-footed, smart, confident, and fast in case of a stampede.

Open range: Land that wasn't fenced in. In Erwin Smith's time some ranching was still done on the open range, rather than on fenced-in pastures.

Outlaw: A steer or horse that ran free on the open range and became difficult to handle.

Railhead: A point on a railroad at which the line either begins or ends.

Range boss: Cowboy in charge of the whole range operation.

Remuda (ray-moo-dah): A Spanish word meaning "relay of saddle horses." This was the term adopted to refer to the large herd of extra horses gathered for use on roundups or trail drives. Each cowboy had a string of six or more cowponies that he could use. The remuda was a combination of all the cowboys' horses.

Round up (verb): To collect cattle into a group by riding around them and driving them into a controlled area.

Roundup (noun): A gathering together of scattered cattle.

Roundup boss: Cowboy in charge of the roundup.

Roundup, fall: A roundup to separate the beeves from the other cattle through the process of cutting. Cowboys would round up the herd, then select the beeves, using their cutting horses to separate them out.

Roundup, spring: A roundup for branding new calves before they got too large and wild to throw and hold down for branding.

Saddle horse: A horse trained to wear a saddle and carry a rider.

Sourdough biscuit: A biscuit made of dough that is in the process of fermenting. The cook would keep a batch of sourdough the whole time, then use a bit each time he wanted a starter to help dough rise for bread.

Stock tank: A small man-made body of water used to water cattle.

Stray man: A cowhand sent to gather his ranch's stray cattle from other herds at roundup time.

String: The group of saddle horses that a cowboy had in the *remuda*.

Tarp: A large piece of canvas used for protecting exposed objects.

Tejanos (tay-ha-nos): Hispanic Texans.

Trail boss: Person in charge of the trail herd to market. On the trail drive, the trail boss would select the spots where the noon break and evening campsite would be set up.

Trail drive: The process of moving the beeves from the range to the market.

Tripod: A three-legged stand on which a camera is mounted to steady it for taking pictures.

Turn out: To get out of bed.

Vaquero (vah-care-o): A Mexican cowboy. Before Texas became a state, it was Mexican territory. Some of the earliest cowboys in Texas were *vaqueros*.

Wrangler: A boy, often too young to handle cattle, hired to herd the *remuda* on roundups or trail drives. The wrangler was also the cook's assistant. He dried and put away dishes, took care of camp gear, and helped to gather firewood.

Yearling: A horse, cow, or any animal that is one year old.